Dear Parents:

W9-AXU-594

Congratulations! Your child is taking the first steps on an exciting journey. The destination? Independent reading!

STEP INTO READING® will help your child get there. The program offers five steps to reading success. Each step includes fun stories and colorful art or photographs. In addition to original fiction and books with favorite characters, there are Step into Reading Non-Fiction Readers, Phonics Readers and Boxed Sets, Sticker Readers, and Comic Readers—a complete literacy program with something to interest every child.

Learning to Read, Step by Step!

Ready to Read   Preschool–Kindergarten
• big type and easy words • rhyme and rhythm • picture clues
For children who know the alphabet and are eager to begin reading.

Reading with Help   Preschool–Grade 1
• basic vocabulary • short sentences • simple stories
For children who recognize familiar words and sound out new words with help.

Reading on Your Own   Grades 1–3
• engaging characters • easy-to-follow plots • popular topics
For children who are ready to read on their own.

Reading Paragraphs   Grades 2–3
• challenging vocabulary • short paragraphs • exciting stories
For newly independent readers who read simple sentences with confidence.

Ready for Chapters   Grades 2–4
• chapters • longer paragraphs • full-color art
For children who want to take the plunge into chapter books but still like colorful pictures.

STEP INTO READING® is designed to give every child a successful reading experience. The grade levels are only guides; children will progress through the steps at their own speed, developing confidence in their reading.

Remember, a lifetime love of reading starts with a single step!

For soccer stars Cora and Riley
—C.B.C.

© 2019 Viacom International Inc. All rights reserved. Published in the United States by Random House Children's Books, a division of Penguin Random House LLC, 1745 Broadway, New York, NY 10019, and in Canada by Penguin Random House Canada Limited, Toronto. Nickelodeon, Nick Jr., Sunny Day, and all related titles, logos, and characters are trademarks of Viacom International Inc.

Step into Reading, Random House, and the Random House colophon are registered trademarks of Penguin Random House LLC.

Visit us on the Web!
StepIntoReading.com
rhcbooks.com

Educators and librarians, for a variety of teaching tools, visit us at RHTeachersLibrarians.com

ISBN 978-0-525-64735-5 (trade) — ISBN 978-0-525-64736-2 (lib. bdg.)

Printed in the United States of America   10 9 8 7 6 5 4

Random House Children's Books supports the First Amendment and celebrates the right to read.

nick jr.

nick jr.
Sunny Day™

JOIN THE TEAM!

adapted by Courtney Carbone
illustrated by Susan Hall

Random House 🏠 New York

It is time to play soccer in the park!

Sunny, Rox, and Blair get special soccer hairstyles!

Rox kicks.

Junior passes.

Blair blocks.

Doodle cheers!

7

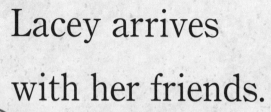

Lacey arrives

with her friends.

She challenges
Sunny's team
to a game.

The game begins.

Lacey takes the lead.

She wants to win
no matter what!

Lacey borrows

a hairpin from Sunny.

She uses it
to deflate the ball!

Sunny does not give up.

She inflates the ball
with her hair dryer!

Rox scores a goal.

Now Lacey is worried.

Lacey tries to cheat.

She rips a hole

in the net.

But Sunny fixes the net
with some hair ribbon.

The score is tied.

Time is running out!

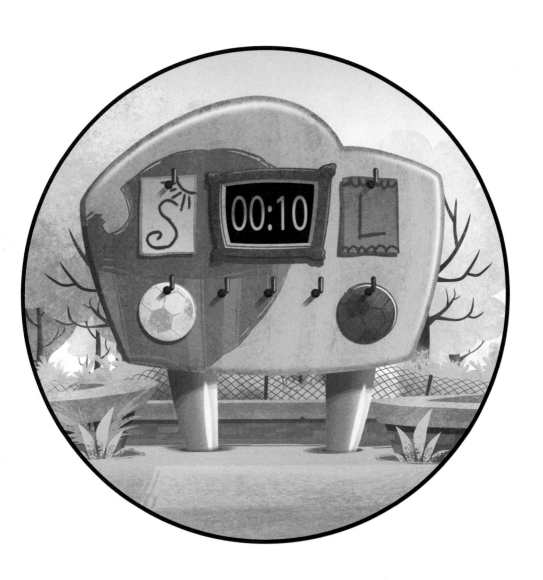

Sunny kicks the ball
as hard as she can.

Goal!
Sunny's team wins!

Lacey sighs.

It was a good game.

She shakes hands
with Sunny.

What a great day!

What a great team, too!